Duck's Vacation

GILAD SOFFER

Feiwel and Friends
New York

A FEIWEL AND FRIENDS BOOK
An Imprint of Macmillan

DUCK'S VACATION. Copyright © 2015 by Gilad Soffer. All rights reserved.
Printed in China by South China Printing Co. Ltd., Dongguan City, Guangdong Province.
For information, address Feiwel and Friends, 175 Fifth Avenue, New York, N.Y. 10010.

Feiwel and Friends books may be purchased for business or promotional use.
For information on bulk purchases, please contact the Macmillan Corporate and Premium Sales
Department at (800) 221-7945 x5442 or by e-mail at specialmarkets@macmillan.com.

Library of Congress Cataloging-in-Publication Data Available

ISBN: 978-1-250-05647-4

The artwork was created with colored pencils and graphite pencil on paper.
Book design by Patrick Collins

Translation from Hebrew by Rena Rossner and Ilana Kurshan
Feiwel and Friends logo designed by Filomena Tuosto

Originally published in Israel by Am Oved, February 2013
First U. S. Edition: 2015

1 3 5 7 9 10 8 6 4 2

mackids.com

To Adi

How relaxing. Just me and the sea.
The perfect vacation.

Whoa! What just happened?
Who turned the page?

There, it happened **again.**

Oh. It's **you.**
Listen, I'm on vacation and
I don't want anyone to bother me!

Do. Not. Turn. Any. More. Pages.

No matter what!

So you turned the page anyway!?

Look, when I'm on vacation,
I want to stay on the same page.
To relax in my chair.
To enjoy the beauty of nature.
See? Look at that lovely bird....

OUCH!

That's exactly the reason
I didn't want you to turn
any more pages.

Give me a break.

All I asked for was
some peace and quiet.

BUT YOU CAN'T STOP

TURNING THE PAGES!

Fine, fine. Turn the pages all you like.

It doesn't matter to me any more.

It can't possibly get worse.

Oops.

Hey, wait a minute...
things are looking up!
I could stay on **this** page forever....

Oh, no!
This would be the **perfect**
time to **turn the page!**

Okay, this is where
I draw the line.
I demand to
return to page one!

This is the last time
I'm going to say it:
Stop turning pages!

He's really getting outta here.

Was it something we said?

No worries, friends. We sail on. Ahoy!
Great treasure awaits!
Adventures on the high seas...

Hey, wait a minute!
Don't close the book!
Our story is about
to begin....

The End

Note: We wish to inform you that when warranted,
the duck was replaced by an experienced stunt double.
Rest assured that no harm came to the duck
during the creation of this book.